"Before I formed you in your
mother's body I chose you.
Before you were born
I set you apart to serve me."
—*Jeremiah 1:5 NIrV*

I Am a Promise
ISBN: 978-0-941565-01-0
Copyright © 2002 by Gloria Gaither
Illustrations copyright © 2002 by Kristina Stephenson

Requests for information should be addressed to:
PO Box 737, Alexandria, IN 46001

I Am a Promise words by William J. and Gloria Gaither. Music by William J. Gaither. Copyright © 1975 Hanna Street Music. All rights controlled by Gaither Copyright Management. Used by permission.

Editor: Barbara J. Scott
Interior Design: Lisa Workman
Art Direction: Laura Maitner

Reprinted 2012
Printed in Mexico

06 07 08 09 • 10 9 8 7 6

I Am a Promise

Written by Gloria Gaither
Illustrated by Kristina Stephenson

GAITHER
music group

"Wow, you've been everywhere, Grandpa!" Jeffrey said.

"Yeah!" his friends agreed.

"Someday," Grandpa said, "if God wants you to, you'll go to faraway places too. All of you will grow up to be everything God wants you to be."

"Really? You mean . . ."

"You can go anywhere
that he wants you to go."

"And I can be anything that he wants me to be."

"I can know anything
that he wants me to know."

"You can know anything
God wants you to know."

"Well, I can climb
the high mountain."

"I can cross the wide sea."

"I'm a
great big promise you see."

"I am a promise. I am a possibility."

"I am a promise, with a capital P."

"I am a great big bundle
of potentiality."

"And I am learnin' to hear God's voice."

"And I am tryin'
to make the right choices."

"I'm a promise to be . . .

anything God wants me to be."

"She's a promise to be . . .

anything God
wants her to be."

"I am a promise to be . . .

anything God
wants me to be."

Now *you* say it...

"I am a promise to be..."

anything God wants me to be."

"With every baby born, children,
God makes a promise to the world.
You are no exception!
No matter who you are or where you live,
your life holds wonderful promises
to bless the family of God
in a way that only you can!
You are special!"

"Even me?"

"You bet! God loves you
very, very much.
Why, you're a promise
with a capital P!"

"I know the plans I have for you," announces the LORD.
"I want you to enjoy success. I do not plan to harm you.
I will give you hope for the years to come."
—*Jeremiah 29:11 NIrV*